THE ARTISTIC SPY

First Published in 2021

Beyond The Vale Publishing

Jackson Molepo

THE ARTISTIC SPY

I dedicate this book to my living father who has given me not just the opportunity to live but the qualities to become a better man.

I dedicate this book to my mother who had and still has the best belief in me to become someone great.

I dedicate this book to my grandfather and his father before him, through their struggle to lead and show great leadership within my community.

NOTE FROM THE AUTHOR

This is a story about nothing.

What is nothing? Nothing is defined as a "quantity of no importance", in this story nothing benefits knowledge, knowledge which impacted lifestyle and experiences which led to the death of a sovereign leader who changed existence. This is a story of a man called Noskcaj Pheri Opelom.

He always considered himself as nobody in the world and saw no importance in his life. He felt like he was not part of humanity but part of a dream that can never exist. He had never killed before, but inside he did kill himself slowly. As he reached manhood he decided to steal his own story and make it another person's story and in return he was able to live an imaginary life. As he progressed to fight existence, he would repeat the same words to his creations. "It's a hard life, sometimes I don't know how I am going to make it, and somehow I am still breathing. I have no one to believe in and there is nothing inside me. It always makes me think every night is the last because when I made you, it was not out of thought but from the unknown."

The book addresses different topics in different chapters with different characters linking them to one another and to one individual. For example, chapter one explains and introduces a life story of Noskcaj and a secret agent who betrayed him, the agent steals information about the most important pictures in the world. Chapter two goes even deeper into Noskcaj's life story and the book goes on to explaining how an artist incorporated with entrepreneurial characteristics gets a job as a registered psychologist, how a businessman fascinated with the number four (4) is betrayed by the number and it ends in a battle of immortals, 'so many battle field scars on the same night was his only wish to become immortal' as we reach deeper into chapter 14.

This is a book for all. All age groups, educating the world about what it means to be stuck in your own life and how it feels to create something only to lose it in a blink of an eye. "I want to paint a portrait, a picture that I will share with my past ancestors, a picture that I will tell my future to never sell, a picture that will remind no one of me and remind me of everyone who ever existed," Noskcaj Pheri Opelom said. "What is this? Is this hope, optimism, wishful thinking, or purely nobody who got lucky and created greatness by mistake? Or maybe nobody is trying to be somebody through imagination?"

We misunderstand and misread stories, facts and opinions, ideas and comments, compliments and statements that others try to communicate or project to us. But what has been said, we choose to hear or ignore simply because of interest or lack thereof. Thinking can involve an undirected flow of ideas, concepts or plans that are not necessarily productive, but can symbolically fulfil ones dreams or the reserve, leading to impractical solutions to problems. I have been trying to write about the highlights of my life. It turns out thinking back and trying to write about my life requires application. Every time I think about writing a book about you, I start understanding where I come from, in all categories.

CHAPTER 1 – I AM A REAL SPY

My pictures have valued me. They are pictures that remind me of everything. They are pictures that describe to me everything and they are pictures that never reminded people about anything.

My name is Noskcaj Opelom and I am from Opelomag. When I was young I believed I was born from royalty, I believed I was born to rule only to discover that my unknown prospective historical origins have been thrown away by a man no one really knew. A man who is forever sleeping peacefully or unpeacefully somewhere in the earths ground or surface. My grandfather's father, who went to war as king and never came back.

I dedicated my life to changing the past, so I created five paintings which could show me how to alter history The first painting I named "THE ARTISTIC SPY". It is a painting of a man called Irehpmam sitting in a designed chair specifically made only for him. A woman stands by his side. She helped him but didn't really believe in him. There are two birds which never got along and a place everyone called "Mostrit".

The most important parts of the painting were the roses behind Irephama, the knife in his hand and his right foot inside the water full of fish. Killing yourself is different from being murdered, but there is a conspiracy that when you commit suicide you delay yourself from God's plans meaning you are thrown into a different world where you are able to make changes. This painting shows two unborn babies printed on Irehpmam's armour.

"I know what you did Ozme," shouted Noskcaj. Ozme was a retired private first-class soldier who fought for two countries and was once a close friend to Noskcaj.

"I am a real spy, I make it a habit of doing things people say I cannot do. I make it a habit of being a person people say I will never be or become," Ozme replied.

The second picture was named *"THE TEMPTATION".* It is a picture of two apples, a flower, four naked women, a city, half face of a woman, designer mansion and a bridge. It is a picture that cannot be connected to the story written for its description. Apart from the information projected on the pictures, Ozme discovered that there was more to the paintings than the eye can see and now he wants all of them. The first picture he stole was *"THE TEMPTATION"* and since then he grew an obsession and knowledge about all the paintings produced by Noskcaj.

"You will not get away with it Ozme," said Noskcaj.

"What the mind believes and imagines is not a world of reality but a world of mere imagination. The bible speaks about a woman called Eve, who seduced a man called Adam to take an apple and eat it from God's garden. This enabled them to see what was not intended for them, no I have tasted the apple you made," replied Ozme. "I walked through fire blinded by acid

11

from melting steel, jumped from the tallest mountain using nothing but plastic bags and broke both my back and neck upon landing on the rocks. And I still had to prove to myself that I am the best living soldier ever made. Finding out secrets about art has always proven to be a signal system communication embedded in my brain and now I want all your paintings, everything you ever produced," continued Ozme.

Before describing the rest of the paintings, the history and relationship between both Nosckaj and Ozme is imperative to outline. They met at a learning academic institution where they both studied psychology. They had one thing in common and that was starting a business together. They never saw value in what they were studying, but taking art and making it a business was a plan they both agreed on.

But they were separated after finishing college when Ozme moved to a different country, leaving Nosckaj to pursue the goal and make reality out of a dream.

The third painting was entitled *"WHERE DO YOU THINK YOU COME FROM?"* It is a painting showing the face of Irephamam, a lion's head, a male and female elephant, the continent of Africa with a baby inside it, music instruments, the rest of the world painted in black and a man working in the continent of Europe. It also shows the country of America lit up by a gun light and a commander being saluted by soldiers.

"This painting is mine! Generations will be wiped out because of your cowardly acts to not hand it over. Names will be forgotten Nosckaj, my obsession has grown wild and this painting has expanded my universal thought, My wife died after jumping from our fast moving jet, she got hit by a 747 aircraft mid-air as she was tumbling down," shouted Ozme.

"I was not aware you were married," Noskcaj replied.

"I am still married and that's not the point here. The point is why she died on that day. She died because I have grown an obsession! She died because I searched every corner of the world looking for art you created from the thoughts and ideas I shared with you. I had to choose whether to save the love of my life or have that painting. And I chose the art. I killed hundreds of innocent people by driving a truck off a bridge on top of a moving train just to get my hands on the second picture. Nothing kills me and I want all the paintings," said Ozme.

"The world we know, Ozme, is different from what we knew twenty years ago. The first person ever to be born or made is a mystery to everyone, but the pictures have shown us historical images no one has ever thought of seeing. Now we know the power of my creations, this is information not meant for any living being, I have found what I was looking for, let us distort these paintings because they are not meant for us," Noskcaj said.

The one picture less important than the rest was a painting of a dancing woman, a man sneaking and picking, and another man looking to the right with an eagle feather on his head., Its name was *"DEAD THORN TREE"*. Noskcaj continually warned Ozme to stop but Ozme had already found this painting. He was left with two painting to complete the cycle of obtaining all five paintings.

"You will destroy everything! Existence will cease to exist. We were friends once and I believe we are still friends so I am pleading with you to return the paintings you stole from me," said Noskcaj to Ozme.

"I'm now immune to all types of poison. I have killed myself but every time my mind refuses to die and my body always come back. These creations have made me taste unimaginable power. I don't need anyone's permission to save the world, and I don't need anyone's permission to create the world I want," Ozme wrote back.

A man who has no desires envisions and directs his ambitions on to nothing and nothing exists in every painting ever made. The fifth and last, but not least painting is a painting of a leader going to war with only his stick and his horse while everyone else attacked in modern tanks, fighter jets, war ships and submarines., It was named *"RIVALRY OF MAN"*.

"When I lay my hand upon *"THE ARTISTIC SPY"* and *"RIVALRY OF MAN"* my task will be complete," declared Ozme.

These were the two painting he could not find no matter what he did.

"No one will stop me, not even you, creator. Nothing will kill me. I am a real spy Noskcaj and I will find them," said Ozme as he walked away from Noskcaj, vowing that he will find the last remaining paintings.

Noskcaj had an incomplete painting, Ozme was not aware of *"FLOWERS GROW IN WALLS"*; its importance would be realised soon enough.

CHAPTER 2 – LOVE IN THIS LIFE

Before Noskcaj started obsessing about the past he had one desire he could not accomplish, and this was love. He had never properly loved someone before and the absence of desire came into his life, living him with a huge space to pursue other things that contributed to his state of existence.

He was a student once and, a student's love in this life can tell a story about temptation. Behind the original drawing of *"THE ARTISTIC SPY"* is a picture of a young woman, this was a woman who loved Noskcaj. She never stopped loving him and the special moments they enjoyed together he excommunicated from his memory and pushed her away, and that was very hurtful to her.

"All I was trying to do was to see if you still love me the way you used to and the way I still love you," she wrote to him once.

Her name was Retina, and they met when they were still young. So, if the woman behind the painting is Retina then who is the woman standing next to Irephama? She had played a very big role in his life because Noskcaj told everyone that she was the one who assisted him in making the impossible possible.

When a normal boy falls in love at a young age he tries almost anything to be with the girl, but Noskcaj was not a normal boy. He never learned to live a normal life, he lived with loneliness inside him and for someone who managed to isolate himself from good, he was a proud boy with a huge ego.

He never understood his behaviour. There was nothing but trauma and anxiety triggered by arrogance and misunderstanding of love, he thought. His personality and believes where seen as abnormal, he believed he was inferior. He spent his life avoiding danger, and he believed that fortune does not always favour the bold.

He told Retina once, "Look inside my eyes, remember when you cried for me when you were supposed to live in my residence at Vidaco (Noskcaj's first academic institution). No one has ever done that for me. I will never forget you, but you have moved on now and I have developed differently."

Noskcaj never fitted in anywhere. No social situation seemed to suit him. He gave up easily because he thought someone else deserved whatever he was willing to give up.

"I have to respect you not coming back into our life. These are expectations that can kill a simple woman like me. No one understood you, but I understood you better than everyone. Love makes its way back around all the time. You never learned how to talk to yourself. I did not either, but I knew how to control your temptations. Every day I would listen to you blame your previous generations for denying you what you believed rightfully belonged to you. What I did not know was that it was a strong addiction! I will always love you however you are, wherever you are." said Retina to Noskcaj.

"Your blood will forever flow inside my veins; I will never forget you," replied Noskcaj.

Noskcaj's social abilities where motivated by his academic life, while his artistic abilities came without lesson - he was a natural in sketching ideas.

"We always thought we would get married one day. I wish I could tell you this in person so I can hug you and kiss you for one last time," he wrote to her. Retina never responded and that was the last time they communicated.

Without expectation, things started to change and Noskcaj decided to continue painting. He thought if he painted differently something positive might emerge, but nothing stays the same. He pained but nothing came out of the work he did. He decided to stop and try a life of love again, so he met another woman, her name was Retina.

They met at a park where Noskcaj was sitting on a bench having a conversation with a friend and she was sitting under a tree reading a book. He failed to say anything to her a few times. He knew he liked her, and he knew she liked him back.

He felt it but decided to count the ways of approach first. He did and the fourth way got him the girl (he went to her pretending he was looking for a place to stay and it worked).

The relationship continued for months until Noskcaj noticed something about himself. He noticed that things had changed and that he had developed a different way of thinking. He saw things differently from everyone else and due to that they slowly moved apart from each other. The relationship between him and Retina stayed even when she was gone.

He felt like there was nothing between him and Retina, he did not understand why he was unable to live life anymore.

"With fire in my bones I did the only thing I knew well, I ran, I ran as fast as I could, I gave up on her." He screamed to himself as he ran. "I don't know what love is, Retina, but I want you to know that it was you all along who created a hole in my heart. It was you who created my temptations. When I first met you, I had a feeling we were not meeting for the first time."

Ozme, on the other hand, always had illusions about who he fell in love with. He was never in one place for a long time. He was charming, charismatic and full of self-pride. He mastered a way of marrying, only to neglect later. A personality built on self-pride; that was Ozme.

Unlike Ozme, Noskcaj had different traits within and unlike Ozme he was told all his life that he will never amount to anything, and he started believing that. His upbringing created a schizophrenic man, and temptations grew within. He fell in love with art and he named all his paintings. Those who had the opportunity to be around him saw him speak to the paintings.

Retina overheard him once. She was confused and thought he was practising a romantic speech for her.

"I had to find you, tell you I need you, my heart now belongs to you," he said to one of his paintings. Art denied him an opportunity to live, denied him an heir (son). He started thinking about the first baby to ever been born, but only saw a picture of a baby imbedded inside 'Africa' as it would in its mother's womb. And thus created his third painting, *"WHERE DO THINK YOU COME FROM".*

He resented the knowledge gained from his art because it led him to understand the reason he could not have a child. He was always sad about this. Retina found him again and this time, she stood next him, to see if he would notice her presences, but he never did, instead he continued.

"Hello I hope I'm not disturbing you, but I saw you across the room. My plan was to ask you if you could be a child and I will be a father so I can understand what this thing love is. I was moved the first time I saw you, I felt like 'who is that?', 'what does he do?' I saw quality in a room full of beauty and I asked myself, who is going to further my obsession of finding the truth? Temptation is the act of influencing by exiting hope or desire, but the way I feel created the war between Juliet and Romeo, now this guy hates me, and I told him I am an artist. He never believed me, and Juliet says I was not even romantic. She is a 'heart breaker' that one!

The desire to be seduced has led a lot to their demise.

"Oh my god, there is a woman at a party and she is shooting people, she desires things that she knows she can never have, she goes for them anyway. She is nothing but a distraction in most people's lives. It will be safe to hate her." This is Noskcaj talking to *"THE TEMPTATION"*.

The painting became famous around the world and Noskcaj became very wealthy after revealing it to the public; people loved it. He became a businessman, and that's when he met Eolifer, his third girlfriend.

"I gave my number to the world trying to give it to you. Did I drive you away? My heart is yours." Eolifer overheard him speaking to his picture in the art gallery, and behind him was a man listening and watching.

Instead of asking him why he was talking so passionately to a painting, she asked him what he sees in that picture.

Noskcaj responded to her and said: "As human beings everyone has an individual life, and it is sometimes intentional that people make decisions to have their mind influenced by art. My wildly love for art was born inside me for a reason."

She was confused so she said to him: "A mind that is influenced by what the person desires is an imitation of an individual who is either himself mentally unfit or he is out of his mind".

Now *"THE TEMPTATION"* was maximised by Eolifer, and the addiction was getting worse and strong inside Noskcaj. "I want to paint portraits, pictures of things that don't exist, pictures that remind my mind that nothing created me," Noskcaj said.

The man behind Noskcaj, was Ozme and when they met again after twenty years apart, his social life started to change, distortion of reality kicked in, disturbance of thoughts and morality barriers took effect immediately after seeing Ozme.

The painting *"THE TEMPTATION"* is one of the most important paintings ever produced by Noskcaj. It should not be destruction but should help solve the temptation within us. The story of temptation is always a result of loss and finding where the question lies has resulted in a lot of people becoming slaves to what they desire most.

"The world you seek to undo the mistakes that you made is different from the world where the mistakes were made. You are the world that you created and when you seek to exist, this world that you have created will also seek to exist."

CHAPTER 3 – I UNDERSTAND WHAT YOU SAID

Success in 'reading' the paintings is a function of the time spent on understanding the creation of man. If you over study the pictures you will never understand them and if you initiate studying them and you do not reach the end, you will never get another opportunity to understand them and make them work.

With most books or other artworks, you start and end wherever you desire.

"Reading my paintings is a process of bringing meaning to the hidden structures of each individual picture," (i.e. bringing the knowledge and understanding of the placement of everything on each painting which creates a picture in your mind in relation to the information in the drawing).

A good reader of this art concentrates not on individual understanding of everything drawn, but also on sound. He who has a superior sense of hearing comes across a picture of something that makes a sound, or words that give meaning to the picture. Incorrect observation and understanding is worse than the shifts that the pictures are capable of doing when brought together in one room.

"Thinking can involve an undirected flow of ideas, concepts or plans that are not necessarily productive, but can symbolically fulfil ones dreams or the reserve". The pictures can lead to impractical solutions, such as why existence exists.

Ozme started learning and understanding them from the way Noskcaj spoke to them, which created a world of images for him, full of opportunities to answer what he didn't really understand. He became obsessed. When Ozme activated *"THE TEMPTATION"* for the first time he was not able to read the painting but he was able to use it.

A strong memory of the paintings depends on the health of information in your subconscious mind and vitality of your brain. The ability to remember every single detail on each painting increases the nature of a universe you want to imagine and your brain creates habits that no living being have ever experienced.

Devoting time to knowledge of these paintings will reduce your own time to live but increase the time of your existence. If you start understanding them, they start understanding you and everything else will follow. It is advisable to always know what to say when explaining each painting or else you will end up unintentionally trading them without intention or knowledge, which leads to the destruction of whatever you have started.

You will end up asking yourself the same question until you die: "Is there a word for half afraid and half angry? can I settle for that due to my inability to complete the task"?

In this current world we remember each other's words, so it is important to tread lightly. Have you ever found yourself saying something but you don't know what you are saying? This is you describing or explaining the paintings (Transcendence).

The brain will create the most important weapon to ever exist, and the brain cells will be locked in a prison of imagination and reality. You will be able to read a planet from start to end in a day, and your time and attention will be devoted to gaining inexistent knowledge, unwanted images and your language will be understood by everything and everyone.

CHAPTER 4 – I AM YOUR MOTIVATOR

Preparing early so that Noskcaj had more time to think about what he missed was one of the inspirations for creating drastic art.

"Will I achieve what I hoped for?" he asked himself. I think the answer lies with what I do to achieve the goals of what I am creating. Hopefully I will be changing *"THE TEMPTATION"* to appeal to what God has created. If I can set up a theory that is realistic in its simplicity, it will explain why creation has influenced man to eat the forbidden apple in the Garden of Eden.

The result of the man's betrayal to God was that he became aware of things not meant or intended for his thought (e.g clothing: no animal wears clothes, man is created in the image of God and when he was created he was made to be different from other living beings, he was created to never be aware of his nakedness, and unlike animals who are not aware, he was tempted to disobey, he was tempted to see what he did not understand.)

There were things God never intended him to understand, but from the naked snake to a naked woman he understood what was not meant for him. *"THE TEMPTATION"* is a painting portraying different naked woman, a face of a woman, two apples with a message written inside them, a designed building and a city, and a flower.

There is a generality that there is a good chance that the theory I'm about to indulge could be correct. I respect the minds power over the body, words and language have been able to motivate and influent a huge number of every living creature on earth.

Before creating all my pictures, I stopped taking risks because I was afraid to fail. I never tried harder until I was told who I was, and what I should have become. So I sat down and looked at the world and all I saw was art. I created a personal emotional strength through imagination; it allowed me to access my unconscious thoughts without influence. I fetched a pencil and through awareness I found courage and motivation through drawing my thoughts.

Before I start a sketch I would ask myself, should I think before I act? and what if I did already?

But what came to mind every time was I knew what I was supposed to draw. You are thinking what they say most of the time.

I didn't know what my father meant, "I will explain when I come back" he always said.

I started having conversation with myself, I never knew how before and every time I opened my eyes I asked myself what I was doing and why am I talking to nothing.

"Let me not negotiate with fear in our heads," I said to myself.

"Because fear is the one who brought me to you," replied the one inside.

"The things you want me to see will give me a purpose to pursue what is not right," replied Noskcaj to himself.

At first, I was intimidated by the quality of the drawings, and when I painted them I saw magic. I started taking a fresh look at everything that come my way, I thought to myself that life can be very easy and enjoyable everyone will be united in my imaginations.

"With my imagination we can change the past, make it a batter place for all, where everyone lives the same, where everyone is their own leader," he told himself.

This thought encouraged him to ask two questions to his imaginary self: "will the future be like this? How will it look like when the past has been altered?" But at that point Noskcaj was motivated to achieve his destiny and not concerned about the future. "Passion leads to imagination and imagination leads to innovation, combine them with more of education then reality is created."

You develop concepts by relating them to what you have heard, read or, seen before. I developed them from nothing. I have no desire for self-promotion, that is something not hidden in my hopes. Every time I tried having positive thoughts, whatever I drew disappeared and then I would discover that I was not paying attention to what I was drawing. It is important to note that *"DEAD THORN TREE"* is based on good luck, something Noskcaj never experienced, so how can good luck exist (what is good luck?).

He told himself that if something is impossible there must be a way of doing it. Tapping into the past was his main objective, so he did something while doing nothing. He had confidence in his abilities and this confidence steamed from past successes of his ancestors. He knew he was from a long generation and he wanted to see each individual who have lived through the years from inception (from the first one). Willing to find out and understand how others from his blood line saw the world and how they recognised themselves whenever they had a narrow-focused life.

Humans have discovered ways to see the future, enabling them to change the future in the present, Noskcaj on the other hand have made it possible to realistically be with each and every male ancestor from the inception of life. He felt like he deserved to know all of them. He needed to know if they risked, if they failed before trying, and if they made their voice heard by the world as to who they were. It is quite important that no man can walk out of his story and Noskcaj was motivated to understand, see and experience the stories of those who are responsible for his existence.

"I will live my mark but first I want to see where all of them left their mark."

The first person to help Noskcaj was himself, but he drew someone on a thrown. He was prepared and he did get the opportunity on that chair but he never got lucky enough to stay. He was constantly fighting and living inside the art, dying and coming back to life every time.

The pictures worked perfectly when they were all together in one room but he was afraid that this cycle of perfection might be broken one day and the art will be a result of unknown and unexpected catastrophic disaster for the world. The art work has a significant impact on the existence of the world and most importantly the universe.

So every time he studied the paintings they progressed to lead him to do what he created them to do. He started separating them, hiding them in different locations around the world, and every time before he would place each painting in its spot his concentration gave up.

On the other hand, Ozme was observing his moves and without wasting time he went for the first painting. "If you really want the change, start by reading the art inside you".

Noskcaj was brave to peacefully create at the level of God's thinking. He never judged but he knew he would have never known if it wasn't for his father's story about his grandfather's father. Without that story he would have not made up his mind about who he was and he would have died not knowing his state of existence.

"Let's show our ancestors that we were not designed, crafted and born for disappointment but born to be kings, crafted by the creator himself. The goal here is not to be afraid of those who are capable of killing the body but appreciate those who sacrificed themselves for the future to exist."

He was determined to complete the universe through art. If he judged he would never had known, because he would have already made up his mind about what he didn't know and all that would have done would be to create distraction; an unguided temptation. It was up to him to show his creation to the world; he was not sure what effect it would have on others

28

or if it would have any effect at all, so he kept the rest to himself and decided to test on painting out of the five.

So, he called his long-time friend and he showed him one picture. He was not sure how he would react.

"So what do you think my friend?" asked Noskcaj.

"This is beyond beautiful. How did you paint this, where did this thought come from?" Ozme replied.

"This is what I have been busy with since you moved to Ecnarf."

"So how many do you have or is it just this one? Twenty years and you have created the best painting ever made," said Ozme.

"No, I have four of them, but I cannot show them to you for now."

"That's fine, but you need to show this to the world my friend, I have the perfect gallery in mind," Ozme said.

He was excited by what he saw, he saw something he never seen before or never imagined of seeing, and Noskcaj noticed that he underestimated the power of the painting. His objective was to study Ozme's behaviour after revealing the painting to him. He thought Ozme saw great art and never thought that there was anything else, so he agreed to display it to the world at Ozme's gallery of choosing.

Ozme was a true born spy he was able to hide his reaction and feeling from the first day he arrived, but when he saw that painting, he taped into a world of extreme passions and more unrealistic images came to his mind, he realised how easy it was to turn them into reality. At the gallery after speaking to

"THE TEMPTATION", Noskcaj turned around only to find Ozme staring at the picture. It became difficult to get his attention.

And for the first time Noskcaj saw the effects of what he created on other individuals, so he came back that evening to take it back from the gallery. The gallery refused and told him it was late and that more than a hundred offers have been placed on the picture, but even when they refused he left the gallery with the painting in his hands.

"No more procrastination, the time has come, the time has come for me to explore all potential dreads, with excitement!" shouted Ozme. "This is the greatest thing the world has ever seen and he has five of them, I have to see the rest. Noskcaj is the smartest human to ever live, I never knew that his patience is better than his pride. He told me about these twenty years ago and I remember the specific words he said to me. 'I am going to create something that will change the world,' he said. And I replied by saying: 'something will push you to get it, giving up is never an option together we shall create something only God can believe'."

To adopt new habits takes repetitive and intentional action, so Ozme dedicated his life, time and effort to pursuing the pictures. He started by offering to buy the paintings from Noskcaj, but he refused, just like he had turned down one hundred and twenty-five offers and all at a minimum of two billion in different currencies.

Noskcaj decided to separate the paintings, placing each one on a different continent and the most important ones in a place where no one dare look for it. Ozme was a retired spy, first class ranked in two countries and he never took no for an answer. He developed ruthlessness and became very wealthy from all the activities he was involved in when he was a soldier. He walked alone at night but walked with everyone else during the day.

However, Noskcaj had walked alone every day and night throughout the years and letting his creations fall into any wrong hands would not happen as long as he still existed.

CHAPTER 5 – WHERE DO YOU THINK YOU COME FROM?

When your father is a freelance research consultant it becomes easy for his son to develop concepts that can change how we see existence. The truth is, every so often comes a man with a very different vision, a man who is able to see the universe in a very different way, a man who understands that if he neglects to share his thoughts with his son, he will experience the same visions until someone late in his line finds the foundation. That one who finds that foundation shall be unable to continue his own blood line.

Noskcaj understood that he would have to simplify his life to focus on the paintings and the things he will sacrifice is for the good of the world. When his father told him about who they were, it was unclear what was expected of him.

"Sorry about that," (as he smiled). "My name is Mr Opelom Noskcaj Irehpmam the second and I will not be subjected to criminal abuse," he said to *"DEAD THORN TREE"*. He now understood exactly where he was from and how he was made to be who he was.

"Sometimes you are not who you think you are in the eyes of others," said his father. "Think about yourself as the last Opelom who outlived Time. If you succeed where we failed you will sit on the chair and you will forever create."

All the paintings share basic concepts designed as images of all those he sought. He will become one who carries around a cane, the cane of Africa; I was the child inside the continent.

The voice of God once warned Noskcaj to not advance with what he was about to do, seconds before initiating the first sketch, but Noskcaj advanced anyway. Pushed by thoughts of finding satisfaction he kept going. Now he created a situation that he shall live to regret, that is if Ozme finds all the paintings. He saw something when creating *"WHERE DO YOU THINK YOU COME FROM?"* He saw two elephants - a big male and a short female - and he spoke to them, thanked them for making him strong all these years, thanked them for grooming him to become an influential figure of life.

"My name is Noskcaj and I will introduce myself today as a topic but before I do that I would like to congratulate one person for reminding human beings that this name will never die; my great grandfather. I am saying thank you to a man who died years before I was born. The world would have not been able to experience my work if he did not reach a certain level in his life, it was not easy for him, I have seen him with my own eyes, he designed a leadership strategy with an approach designed to show me how the world functions. But he did not do it alone, that's why I shall extend appreciation to the soldiers who have helped him and people who listened to him, motivated him and taught him how to be a true Opelom. They have instilled a skill inside him that he has passed through to me and they helped in the craft that will be used to achieve goals and objectives of all worlds."

One Professor of Research referenced Noskcaj during his studies. "I have known Mr. Opelom for the last six months as I was his lecturer. Mr Opelom has performed very well, as is his nature. He is not only performing well in formal assessments but also very willing to contribute towards any discussions. Many of my students often had a problem understanding him when he wanted to articulate a discussion, but for me as a scientist, I did understand him. He indicates willingness to contribute to interactive sessions and has the ability to express himself well in arguments. He impressed me with his determination to succeed in achieving the high results of everything he worked on. He always contributed more than what's expected. His observation skills are good and he has mastered a unique approach suitable for theory discourse. He is also logical in his reasoning. One thing I noticed out of the ordinary about him was that, on his scripts, or any paper document that passed him was a drawing of a horse, he has hidden gifts." That was the perceived opinion of the Professors about Noskcaj.

In 991 my ancestor was born, in April 1991 his descendent was born in Opelomag. At four days old Noskcaj could hear everyone who came to see him as a new born. He understood what it meant when visitors would say he looked like Irephama. At seven years old he drew a picture of a flower (a rose) on his arm, with a sharp broken pen cover. At ten years he drew two birds (doves) on his bedroom wall and at seventeen he drew his face on a blank piece of paper. As the years passed he carried on drawing. One of his past drawings was of two brothers looking at the sunset. Once he completed all of the paintings he gave a name to their combination.

Bocaj is the son of Kcaj, and Noskcaj is the son of Bocaj, and Kcaj's father was Nadroj. A man is free to peruse whatever work he wishes only by the fact that he or his father before him has worked to a greater purpose, even if the work done by different generations of Opelomes may have differed.

It dawnedupon all of them to find the courage to start from the beginning and build their own legacy instead of wanting to inherit it.

Nadroj chose to die in battle only to prove to his previous generation that he deserved his fortunes. If one generation fails to utilise and capitalise on his achievements, he shall fail to lay a foundation of preparation and will show he is simply not worthy or unfit to hold greatness and sit on the Opelom chair. It will not end there. He shall lose the advantage to his future generation to enjoy, but one will rule if the need to do so should arise again.

Noskcaj's father had previously worked as a lecturer, but he never took advantage of what his father stories portrayed. Instead he chose to share some of the stories with students who were not meant to study or hear them. His students never understood him, they did not understand his stories, but his son did. His co-written publications and his thesis on mathematics almost exposed the family secret. He was a senior lecturer in Research Methodology and focused on the upliftment of disadvantaged populations. He meant well and did good. As a renowned researcher, he received the Sought-After award for his exceptional contribution to community upliftment.

In his teenage years Bocaj took Noskcaj and his brother to visit their grandfather's grave for the first time. Noskcaj had flash images of being there years ago as a young boy. He turned around and looked at his brother and said: "I honour my grandfather before him by finishing his work.

I will be an old man unable to continue my work, but one from my brother's sons will finish my work. I shall become nothing in this world but I shall say goodbye to *"THE TEMPTATION"*. That painting did all of us wrong, she took our time, she took my mind and she took their bodies. She has caused me and denied me the chance to know myself and she stole three generations of conscious minds.

Maybe losing her to Ozme may come as a relief of personal emotions, or disaster to the rest. It is unknown what it will do to him; someone who has been in the front line of battles, how will he battle with this painting? The art represents all of them, designed from all their physical and mental expressions. Noskcaj has achieved his ambition, he has done what he saw as right."

I feel very sad, very sad that I might have created a weapon that will bring nothing but struggle. I have no evidence to base my apology on, there are just too many. This has resulted in a combination of stories and good sessions that turn out deadly.

I have been trying to write about the highlights of my life for years and thinking back my life requires application, and every time I think about it I think about how my creators failed and in what categories.

Honour to my father: "A man honours his father but understands the necessity of life and if his father is able to see him become someone in this competitive life he has dedicated his effort to predating the next generation of Opeloms."

CHAPTER 6 – ENTREPRENEURIAL CHARACTERISTICS

The paintings are resources; they are something that one needs to produce, they are something that one needs to influence. The paintings were not his only invention. Before them he had invented something that could determine the psychology of business and the world of invention.

It is important that we understand the analogy that our grandfathers before us worked with their hands. In today's world people work with their brains and for every change to occur and work there has to be someone who invented something.

We live in a world where people are able to provide content that is accessible to millions, unlike followers who were not aware of a king's judgment, a 1,000 years ago due to communication mechanisms.

A man virtually unknown came in to Noskcaj's life during his academics, Oen, who was the owner and founder of a company called Pharis-Lanto. He founded his business alone but with help from Noskcaj they turned it around into a world class business. The brand name was everywhere, in every country and town.

The first day they met, Oen gave Noskcaj a task, which was to introduce a product similar to his, but different. At first Noskcaj never showed interest, he had nothing to prove to Oen but on his way home thirty minutes later he came across a sign in big letters – 'Entrepreneurial Characteristic' and he decided to turn back to Oen's shop.

A week later Pharis-Lanto was a mega company in the country and every week from then the business was run on a new idea, expanding to different countries. They became business partners and created inspiration for the world.

What Noskcaj brought to the company was the only thing that created creativity through greatness and critical thinking. Billions of people recognised the brand and most of them couldn't live life without its innovative technology, food supplies, energy and engineering.

Oen made sure that the real inventor became known and he called it a collective effort. He would unleash a rampage on to a journalist who questioned him about rumours or allegations that the only thing he contributed to the success of the company was the name and starting it, without knowing how to grow and that success started with the introduction of Noskcaj.

On the other hand, Noskcaj's interests were linked with rudiments created by procedures and terms of imaginations and predictions of one number, number four. One of the paintings was a source of power of this number, which he took. This was the primary key factor of the business success.

It is quite important to understand that Noskcaj, as an artist was complex. He had emotions that a lot of people did not understand and most of the time people rejected who he was. Oen insisted that he be the face of the company because of the personality difference.

Noskcaj was a disorderly individual with a confused manner of imagination, but his idealistic images were always impractical until he made them practical, they were impulsive deliberations determined by his introspective thoughts. He always believed in independent work, and he knew that he did not want what everyone else wanted.

Oen wanted more money, more expansion, and more power. This difference in ambition created a conflict of interest between the business moguls. Oen started to realise that Noskcaj was a nonconformist, an original individual without passion or desire for material or sense of achievement. But he knew that he loved art and that all his earning went to some sort of artwork. They slowly drifted apart.

Oen was a great entrepreneur himself. He was adventurous and the business was run like a machine that was programmed to be acquisitive. He was an ambitious individual who depended on others to produce and grow the business, he was strategic in turning ideas into reality and most of the time immediately. His domineering behaviour will prove to be fatal, but it was his exhibitionist tactics of the secret he kept, that destroyed his optimistic plans. Noskcaj did give him a sense of key factors that drove his business success but he did not do so with direct words of indication.

Both Noskcaj and Oen developed concepts that led them to produce the unthinkable. One day Oen was analysing the new concept they had just came up with and he asked himself one question: "How does an artist have entrepreneurial characteristics?"

Psychological studies have shown that individuals can develop characteristics that they were not born with, they can simply learn certain competencies and for someone who is high in optimism experiences better moods when he is able to master characteristic that advanced their imagination.

Oen started investing in a secret personality development program, naming it: "The 4 Learning Process (T4LP)". It would be a program run by four specialists and would be characterised by and recognised in patterns of responses or behaviours that are conditioned or learned and reinforced or rewarded. Through influences one learns from extracting four things from another human being.

Art has become a business in the world today and became one aspect of Opelom's life that will never be turned around. It will be one thing that can be stolen in psychical form, but it shall be impossible to take away its emotional impact. Business is an important part of Oen's life; Noskcaj understood that so he gave him the number to continue and thrive in business.

CHAPTER 7 – I AM NUMBER FOUR (4)

A less self-serving agenda for Oen was an umbrella of his latest investments. One of the specialists called in by Oen was a thoughtful black consciousness artist who never revealed to Oen his love and passion for art. Oen brought him in as a psychologist due to his theory titled 'A story critique with an empowering title'.

T4LP was intended to give individuals the capability to influence a change in behaviour; its mission was to change man to act in accordance with someone else's wishes. The ability to be able to recognise your own skills, values, interests, strengths and weaknesses was a concept the psychologist knew very well.

"It is a legacy beyond comparison if I collectively make reality of this work," the psychologist thought to himself.

He remembered that he used to have goals of ruling his own homeland once and he perceived himself as the authority that stems from being the best at what he does. He knew Oen worked with an individual called Noskcaj. Oen spoke highly about him with one of the four specialists in secret meetings and the psychologist listened avidly. They always said something about 'excellence is a habit' and that Noskcaj was the only living human who have exhibited this kind of character since the test was done four hundred years ago by the Egyptians.

The specialists lived in a secret facility, away from anything and everything that had to do with Paris-Lanto because they were not employed by Paris-Lanto but by its owner for something different.

"Since we will all pass away, and our work lives on and survives, don't you think that leaving our work in Oen's hands is the right choice? Has any of us been told the purpose of what we are working on? I think one of us needs to take a sample once its complete, just until we know that it will not be used to harm but for good. Man will be born and perish without ever knowing that he was controlled his entire life, he will live under an unnoticed rule without knowing," said the psychologist to one of the team members.

The team member was from a different field of study, so he did not see the implications of what they were creating, he was a scientist.

Oen was always giving speeches that articulated dreams, speeches that offered hope, stirred hearts and minds and offered everyone including his staff across the world a vision of a better world through his company Paris-Lanto. Compared to Ozme, Oen did not know much about Noskcaj's paintings but he could feel that there was something Noskcaj was working on.

He remembered listening to him speak about a girl behind a picture, he never understood what he meant. He said he could not figure out the meaning behind her smile, why she was smiling. Oen always wanted to ask him about the drawing but every time he tried, his words created a world not even he could understand. He never understood why, he told the psychologist.

Oen had turned Paris-Lanto in to a lifestyle of individuals to become heroes, champions, kings, rulers, captains and generals, Presidents and CEOs and in return he expanded his wealth, power and influence.

Noskcaj could not live in such a world. "This is a world of the uncontrollable substance of life," he said to himself.

Not understanding and knowing why Oen has such a focus interest in him after he left the company, he could think of only one thing - the objective of knowing everything about the origin of the number. Noskcaj received a letter with no title, no introduction or sender, only a single page with these words:

"What is hard and how hard do I work? The problem with being loyal to a course is that the course will always betray you. I am Number 4 and I am a necessity to the power of invention."

Noskcaj investigated the complexity of the letter's content. He did not have the ability that enabled him to investigate, but they came to him after reading that letter. He knew exactly who wrote the letter, what he didn't know was how he knew about the number.

CHAPTER 8 – BLIND OF AN EYE

When you are in a fight there has to be a loser, but the one who loses can always make his way back. Up until now we understand that Ozme had developed a negative spirit making him a very deadly subject to have to deal with. Noskcaj knew that he had to come up with a counter fight. If Ozme was successful, he will have to find a solution to what he made, maybe even come up with a different project that is opposite to his initial project. If he fails to do so the same interests and addiction would spread inside millions of people and inside most of them it would create something not even Satan himself could approve.

Both Noskcaj and Ozme had the opportunity to see how human behaviour had evolved, they had a chance to speak to some of the first people who walked on earth, but Noskcaj always blamed one painting for showing them a way that he never intended.

When he made it, it was not intended to do what it's capable of doing. "You cannot blame anyone except yourself for what you did, but you did it for us, you will never have yourself back and let me help you see the world the way I see it," said Ozme.

"Are we cursed? We just can't stop!! You plan to stop when you are broken into pieces, but when you get the resources to build yourself up again temptation runs in and you see yourself doing it again. I am failing because I have not completed my task alone, I brought someone in and I pretend to be a title that will withstand destruction. But, I introduced destruction to a spy. My results are not good. Where are you, man? I need you back Noskcaj, I need to be free, I haven't seen myself for a long time and I am feeling pain. This is the year I should be performing better than I have ever performed in previous years. I am failing but I have not failed yet, I was just blinded on my left," said Noskcaj to himself.

No change came and none of them started doing things right. They were both given an opportunity to improve, but one vowed to never stop.

"She is not worth fighting for. Stop messing with my mind, I am quitting while I still have the resources. Opportunities can be messed up because of you and I have seen that She is not worth fighting for, Ozme.Leave her and let me seek out a professional for the liberation of your mind.

She is a serial manipulator and using my resources to stop you. My fight with you is starting to be a hobby to me, but you will always be my motivator. The professor might help."

"Can love be negative? I feel like I don't have it, don't feel it, don't know it, maybe it will find me." He complimented himself while insulting himself, he knew very well that love never grew in his heart, but he tried searching for it again.

"You might lose, love is blind, if it's special it lasts, but what do you really love Noskcaj, what exactly is love to you, what does it mean to you?" Noskcaj asked.

"I keep my feelings far away in my different self."

His definition of love: "I see the same pictures whenever I close my eyes and go to sleep. These pictures lead me to make decisions when I wake up. Whenever I consider an action I ask myself will this decision make the picture? Reality pulls it out of my mind and into the world, so love to me is nothing. It is a quantity of no importance. It is an unclear wave that comes from passion, it lets you think you are in control, progresses your mind to an emotional stage, and for humans it always works out as expected. The truth is, I couldn't tell Retina that I loved her. Reality has a way of pulling thoughts and feelings into the world."

CHAPTER 9 – THE SONG OF BRAGGING DEMONS

"We just want to dance,
we don't want to listen to the lecture,
want to dance,
we want to dance until we lecture,
we just want to dance.

You don't have to say anything about the dance,
just raise the flag and maybe we will come out of our comfort
zone.
I am never relaxed,
I keep fighting demons,
I think I should brag,
I can fix it right here, right now, and we might disappear,
you don't see anything after that, then you are scared.

Over time you hear my name and you pretend,
from now on we are going to do what I want because I am the
only one with no pain,
I keep emptying a wine bottle into the dish of roses, as I
continue singing to you.

I kept on looking at the drink go down the dish,
I wanted to say something,
but I just watched the drink go down.

I was not beautiful any more,
I was not beautiful because I was concentrating on one rose,
they became more beautiful.
I am the scales of justice and the concurred of the pal of death,
sing for the cause sing, sing, sing my love.

We always knew that getting out of a difficult situation
required that you don't give up, and now I shall write a letter to
the priest:

"Hi, priest, I think I made a mistake. I am not a quitter but
I'm deregistering. I am sorry for having to make you go through
this, I know I might be throwing away an opportunity. I always
wanted to be here, but now I am here and all I want is to live. I
have already taken this decision; it might not be the best
decision I have ever made but I appreciate your support and
thank you for everything you did for me. I can't continue. I
thought keeping a positive attitude will make things go my way,
but I am thinking twice.

But before I go tell me who you claim yourself to be me,
thank you for making me feel like I am guilty."

I was walking on the beach once,
I looked back to see what was behind me,
but there was nothing,
not even my footsteps on the sand,

my mind was somewhere else.
I was thinking about my true love, she used to do things that made my head spin,
but the life we live is a justified programme of infidelity.

At one point I wanted to think about everything,
I thought of Freddie Kruger singing in my spa,
meddling with innocent minds,
swearing at kings who are not smart.

Every time he thought about killing he stopped,
and me dating a man who never smiled.
It was to be sent to prison to choke on its own blood.
The poor disgust them because they are us, a shadow of our emotions;
they show us what we look like without our fine clothes,
how we smell without our expensive perfumes.

Your art is a set of dreams beyond our reach,
it is nothing and nothing can be worse explained than something,
and nothing can be or mean something,
but the truth is nothing,
it cannot be better or worse because nothing is just nothing.

My question is how can I believe in something that doesn't exist, something you don't know or never experienced? All you have to say is say maybe the numbers listed in your mind haven't worked in a long time.

You are my song and I sing you with vengeance in my heart.
I am your Retina, and I am surrounded by bragging demons.

CHAPTER 10 – USELESS HOPE

We never looked at things in advance when we were at the lab.

"Will we live while we live if we finish this job?" I asked one of my co-workers.

He replied, "I don't know who you are, and I don't care, we were advised when we started that we shall not have any other conversation outside the work we are here for, please believe me, I will obey Mr. Oen," replied one of the specialists.

"Here take this, it is my first autobiography, the only copy, if you become interested about who I am, along the way read it," said the psychologist.

"Inside the book was a chapter where he spoke about someone he fell in love with."

"I did not get a chance to know you better but I love you. Perhaps I won't be able to write again, I have been sent on another quest, but I need you to know that it is also my integrity that is important, this is the last inch I have, and it is the only inch that is going to set me free. I am hurt with bullets all over my body. I am writing this to you because I love you, I might not know you but I am married to you. When we broke up you became confused and you confessed to my enemies about my life, about who I was. I didn't blame you, because I loved you, I blamed myself for telling you who I was. You couldn't live with the thought of betraying me, so you killed yourself. I am writing to you while I am in a cell, while I know that you are no more.

They came and they found me. I shall not die now. You were the last one worth having, worth living for, and wherever you are I will be coming to take you home. You are my flower, you are my Arolf. I have the painting my love and I shall never give it up. I should have never let you jump from that plane, my heart was somewhere else. We must never let them take what is left from us or else I may never see you again, I hope you accept, I hope the world turns and things get better, I love you and I will be there soon."

The scientist came to his chambers, shut the door, stood there for a minute and asked him: "What was she like?"

The psychologist replied: "She was like perfect artwork, they are beautiful, mysteries, and they both created emotional deprivation. I couldn't stop smiling when she was around, I couldn't wake up when I fell asleep, I could not go out because I wanted to stay. I lost my focus, I was not committed or willing to go back to work, so I stayed, and I fell in love with my target. I concentrated more on love and when she died the mission was complete, but I didn't care about the mission anymore because I had a new objective. Animals use strength, power and ability to get what they want, humans are the same. Human perception is most motivated by achievement; once we notice that we cannot keep something, we sacrifice it so that no one can have it, but if you know a way of getting it back you give it up. I live with these people today and they will be here and the next day they are gone.

This is different for me and my former friend, we will live with ourselves for the rest of our lives. Humans portray themselves as those above the law, laws made by them. They don't understand that authority stems from being the best at what you do. I apologise to God for every sin I ever made. I apologise to God for every sin I am about to commit. I am about to create a different reality through imagination. I know you created man and man betrayed you Lord. I am not every man, but I believe that man is a hero to his own story and in his own right. I am on a set of uncertainty at the moment. Well I have never had no true meaning to its creator. Everyone's dreams are blind, and I am ready to go to war to defend mine. I will spare no-one; no-one will stay at home. I shall invoke useless hope in everyone's hearts, they will give up everything to fight for me, and they should never blame me for creating that hope."

The scientist was baffled, confused and had more questions. "Who are you?" he asked.

When two friends have dated one woman, they create a situation where neither friend can attend each other's burial. Noskcaj and Ozme know how to speak to *"THE TEMPTATION"*, they both have a relationship with this painting, and when two boys fight for one girl, she will, at the end of the fight, live with one of them.

Even when he knew the direct implications of *"THE TEMPTATION"*, he wanted it back. He created it and it still had purpose for his quest. The picture only increased both men's hatred for each other, it widened their separation. It created a situation that if one of them should die, the other should not attend his burial or he himself will die on that day. This shall be a tradition for them and their future generations.

This created a challenge between both men because even if they have become enemies, saying goodbye was honouring your fellow brother's funeral. They made a promise to each other when they were young men, that they shall live to see their goal become reality or they will die together trying.

"What we have surround ourselves with determines what we do? You know you don't belong where you are right now, let me help you destroy her. How long is it going to take to make the decision and show some courage, Ozme? The greatest sin known to man is to miss your mark; I need that painting so that I don't miss mine. I have another painting and she made you aware of it. *"THE ARTISTIC SPY"*, shows a man sitting on a designed chair. The chair has two heads of elephants crafted in front of the shoulder rest, a bowl of roses behind him and a message on the left hand side of the chair. The chair is a peaceful sculpture made by the first Opeloms to revise the effects that man made in the world. That chair is a simple tribute to the Opeloms. Not to outsiders," Noackj said to Ozme.

It is true that the paintings can change lives, and with them in Ozme's position no one is safe. No life will be changed for the best, the mind of a spy is different from an ordinary human, the mind of a spy is a mind of an assassin, a programmed agent controlled to kill at any cost. They are used to living as characters, and once they imitate a certain character they make sure that they never break character until executed with perfection and the task complete. Ozme was a soldier for a long time and a mentality of a soldier trained in two different countries with two different ideologies equals an unpredictable individual.

He wants to use the paintings to kill every living thing from the beginning of life, so that he can re-invent and shape the past according to his wish. This will lead to war; he could not be convinced, as long as he knew what power the paintings have his mind is set and ready to complete the task. He cannot execute his plan because he is short of two paintings to complete the cycle; he now knows that the paintings work only if they are all in one room, close to each other and in perfect order.

Oen's workers around them started noticing changes in the two men but they didn't know exactly what was going on. They noticed because Oen found out the true identity of the psychologist. People started talking about this mythological scenario and they started choosing sides. With three paintings stolen Noskcaj had no choice but to make a deal with Ozme. Ozme was desperate for the last paintings and that was the one big 'peace move' that could change evil events leading to a ruthless existence. If Ozme was to get hold of all paintings the last hope is lost.

CHAPTER 11 – IS THE DEAL IN MOTION?

Ocram and Ecnul are two individuals with unbeatable standards of thinking, and they were also two of the specialists hired by Oen. They were capable of making credible decisions from different levels or field of study.

Ocram was a specialist in the field of Celestial Phenomenon and Biology among others and Ecnul mainly focused in all fields of engineering, but mostly mechanical. All together they included the scientist and the psychologist. Oen instructed them as a last stage of the project to research one individual and find information that enabled the work to be finalised.

Noskcaj hadn't been seen by anyone for more than four months. None of the specialists had met him, except for one. And he who knew him did not want any disturbance in his primary mission. The psychologist had just met them and he found himself in between. They were talking to each other through him, arguing, giving up and making decisions through him.

Noskcaj and Ozme on the other hand had a deal in motion, they shall not communicate until each agrees to the terms. Both have to honour the pact by going into Mostrit and signing the agreement with the blood of their ancestors.

Ocram and Ecnul were two individuals who knew how to solve problems. They placed the psychologist as spokesperson, to represent the group in the quest for information. Ocram also commented that he had confidence in the psychologist and that he was the best fit as an undercover agent. He did the job with flying colours, of course. He went out and came back with information that enabled them to complete the job, but he told them that he did not gather the information from Noskcaj but from something Noskcaj made.

Oen was reluctant to know what this thing was. The product was complete, but it was not in Oen's possession, it was missing and everyone who was working on it was also missing. Noskcaj however took a decision to go to a place called Airoterp. As he knew this was the place where one of his pictures was leading him, he would have a lot of opportunities to make a lot of decisions there, and most of this decision will be influenced by the things that he exposed to life.

Since his arrival in Airoterp he found himself in a situation where he wrote a lot instead of painting. Deals were made with different individuals for him to try find peace for the world, but he knew that first he had to make sure that the primary deal between him and Ozme was finalised and adhered to. There was one thing that would smooth track that deal and that thing is the reason he was in Airoterp.

Oen on the other hand, had lost his prized product and the men who were working on it. He went to the facility where they were working but it was burned down. He suspected one of them, two of them or even all of them had betrayed him and taken the product for themselves, so he initiated a manhunt through all his connections. He gave the authorities pictures of all the men, and informed them that they had been collectively involved in the murder, kidnapping and stealing of company property.

Noskcaj became aware of this. He saw the pictures and he recognised one face, it was disguised but he knew that face. He immediately left but, on his way back he became lost, he kept going until he realised that he was not on Earth anymore, he was on Mars, but how is that possible? How can you leave one place and pitch up in a different world? He did not know that he was the one who asked for this and now the deal is in motion and he is starting to regret jumping into a non-reversible decision.

CHAPTER 12 – INCREASED CHANCE TO BE DECEASED

Change can be difficult for everyone and everything. Noskcaj had an additional picture but it was incomplete, it was still in sketch form and not yet painted.

It was his first attempt to search for the truth. No one knew about it, even he forgot it existed. It was unknown what power it will contribute to the rest of the paintings, so he decided to look for it and destroy it before Ozme found it.

He asked himself one question: "How do you destroy something you killed a long time ago?"

He was only seeing half the truth; he didn't know what kind of power it had if transformed into a painting. He looked to his right and saw a flower - it was green and it was growing on a wall between three bricks. It was at that point that everything became dark.

When he opened his eyes, he was on the edge of a mountain with his hands tied up He looked down and he saw steam, red liquid boiling, it was lava. He looked to his left and there he saw Ozme sitting on a chair with two men standing behind him, one holding a briefcase.

"I need those paintings Noskcaj," Ozme said.

Noskcaj replied: "You don't have to do this friend! The power of my creations was meant for me; you will destroy all of us".

Ozme threatened to throw him in to an active volcano if he didn't disclose where the last painting was. He'd killed 44 people looking for *"RIVALRY OF MAN"*, and found it, but through sacrifice.

"You cannot give dead men their lives back but I can with that painting." He then signalled to his man carrying the briefcase. The man took out one of the stolen paintings and a cable with a needle attached to a small laptop. He stuck the needle into the back of Noskcaj's head, into his brain and placed the painting next to him.

After a while the man shouted: "We have it, I know where it is!"

Ozme stood up and whispered into Noskcaj's ear: "I am a real spy nothing can kill me, thank you for I am evolving."

He then pushed him into the lava and watched him slowly sink in. Noskcaj was dead, vanished - he was nothing now.

Ozme travelled to the middle of the Atlantic Ocean sent two men to dive down and bring everything found on the ocean floor.

The men came back and told Ozme that there was a ship down there, a very old ship. "It looks like it was built thousands of years ago sir, I've never seen anything like it," one of the men said.

"The painting is inside. Call everyone to come here and bring all the equipment!" Ozme ordered.

Four hundred men came on ten ships. They searched the wreck but found no painting. Ozme was angry, ordering everyone to go back and no-one return until the painting was found. One of the men suggested that maybe it is buried under the ship. They tried to flip the ship over for more than 2 weeks. The soldier was right, and now Ozme has all the paintings, or so he thinks!

CHAPTER 13 – FLOWERS GROW IN WALLS

When Noskcaj was thrown in to the mountain full of lava he had in his possession the sketch of his first drawing.

The volcano suddenly stopped boiling and started cooling off, and becoming rock. After an hour the rock became diamonds and started to crack.

'Booooom!'

The whole mountain exploded, rubble flying all over and now the *"RIVALRY OF MAN"* is about to start. War was coming.

When he emerged from all the smoke, from the cooling lava, he was different. Fully dressed in a designer armour with a cloak at his back, a crown on his head and holding a stick.

As he was walking towards the trees in the forest he saw something moving and walked straight towards the moving object. It looked at him with its blue eyes and he looked back. It walked towards him and he reached out and touched it on its head. He climbed onto it and it started to run, it ran so fast that everywhere it passed trees burned, rocks flew all over.

He stopped in the first town, the road behind him was still smoking. He dismounted and entered a restaurant, where he was told that Ozme had taken command of the whole world, and his plans for world domination were almost achieved.

He rallied everyone who was not supportive of Ozme and Ozme was given the news that there was an individual who was rebelling against him. He didn't know who this individual was, but he knew whomever he was, he had some powerful influence.

Ozme sent spies to record Nosckaj, but every time they reported back to him and showed him the video tapes, Nosckaj could not be seen in the videos, he was invisible in every tape. Ozme was furious. He ordered killings of his spies, but every time he sent in more they brought back the same thing, videos and pictures without this person's face. Noskcaj has managed to gather more than one and a half million soldiers ready and willing to fight against Ozme and his army.

Noskcaj brought in war ships, fighter jets, submarines and tanks, everyone was well-equipped. It is time for war, Noskcaj 'The Leader' was going to war with only his stick and riding his extraordinary horse while everyone else attacked with modern technology.

Ozme doesn't know his opponent. His soldiers don't know him and the men fighting for this new leader don't know who he is too. All they know is he has influenced their hearts and made them believe that they are fighting beside a demi-god. In the forest he found that horse and after he touched it, it became part of him, its bones became steel and its skin became tough and after he climbed on to it he gave it a name. He called it Nibor and it can run faster than a jet.

It was time for war.

Everyone was ready, Ozme used the pictures to create a very strong army, he was using the T4LP but he did not know why the pictures couldn't reveal who this guy ready to fight him was.

On the other hand, Noskcaj knew everything about the man he was going into battle with. He was worried about the power Ozme has from the pictures, but he knew that that he did not have the *"THE ARTISTIC SPY"*. People always die in wars, civilians and the innocent get involved, bullets are flying all over, bombs are exploding, and people are vaporized, body parts everywhere and families suffer, and all this was because Noskcaj created abnormal paintings.

There came a time when Noskcaj ended up in front of the barrel of someone who was ordered to shoot, and the soldier fired the whole magazine into his head. His horse charged and killed the soldier. Nothing happened to Noskcaj. He maintained a war effort. In the rubble of men shooting each other, planes and tanks were being overturned and finally they saw each other.

CHAPTER 14 – EVERY AMBITIOUS MOVE IS A GAMBLE

So many battlefield scars on the same night!

Ozme's only wish was to become immortal, it was mandatory but reduced to tears mixed with blood for everyone to see! They were all ready to die using Kidivonte as their military mind was charged by the power of the spirit from the painting.

Noskcaj always played spy, but he was hampered by his horse, who, having been brought back to life had evolved beyond a mere stallion.

Ozme on the other hand was an individual who would break his back to get what he wanted, on and on until the early morning. It is a strong feeling to be in the centre of attention, it makes you understand and question power. The two men saw each other. Neither of them moved and the whole world became dark.

There was no light, no sunshine, no moonlight and not even a sparkle of a star, it was pitch dark. There were still screams and shouting of men in pain, scared and screaming: "I am blind!"

The two men saw nothing but each other, they sized each other up and only one mental picture was visible in each mind – *"THE ARTISTIC SPY"* - and who was sitting on that chair. The painting revealed nothing about war, but life after war.

They both asked themselves, what can one feel when he places his hand on an elephant's head? What is it thinking and why does it keep calm?

They say if you close your eyes you get to think clearly, and when you are provided with an ultimatum to kill or be killed most living will save themselves. Noskcaj was walking, walking towards killing his friend. With Ozme it was simple, he was a spy and he was focused on only one thing; securing all the pictures was his objective, he cared nothing about death.

He always had one question in his mind: what will happen if he killed the man who created the pictures? But his answer came to life when he saw Noskcaj back from the dead. He believed he killed Noskcaj when he threw him into the volcano. His pictures value him, they made him into something he never thought he would become, they are pictures that remind him of everything (all that exists and all that existed), they are pictures that describe to him everything and they are pictures that never reminded people about anything.

Why did he paint them? What was the first thought before he thought of drawing? He was nothing but he evolved and became everything, nothing is not something, so nothing cannot be something that doesn't exist.

"The pictures have valued him," but Ozme is desperate to find out what that means, now he feels like the paintings are part of Noskcaj, and that he cannot be killed. The paintings have made Ozme reach limits he never thought possible. No matter how doubtful, he attacked with strong emotions running through his blood, thinking about nothing but his destiny. He ran towards Noskcaj, sword in one hand and gun in the other, charging along an open battlefield to destroy the opposite force.

There were 10,000 tanks leading Ozme's charge but like a tip of a spear Noskcaj's four hundred combined armies sped across the battlefield behind him, standing fast as the enemy charged toward them.

During their planning before the battle, Noskcaj visualized this moment and decided to inform the commander of his armies that when the enemy attacks and reaches the hills something extraordinary will take place.

However, the commander was distracted by the loss of men and during the foreseen attack his mind blocked everything they had planned during the planning session. When Noskcaj noticed this as he saw the commander charge from the right side, he was faced with a difficult set of choices.

He could have stopped him and his unit, but that will lose them. Time to execute the plan, leaving the crews sitting in the open, subject to enemy fire. The other choice was to keep calm and lose 50 men per minute. He decided to order his men to drive left.

Ozme knew that if they were to attack first they would die quickly, so he was not sure which army to attack first but this whole time his target is locked and moving left, I should have gone right instead. The opposing forces crushed first with the right unit led by commander Noel.

Choosing the direction to face your enemy gives you advantage of measuring the situation, and after you have made your choice there will be no stopping. Guessing which decision is correct can lead to disaster, but upon reflection the commander looked back and saw Noskcaj and asked himself: "How could I have served you well? I have gotten everyone behind me killed, I refused to sit in the open and wait to be slotted. The Commander was crushed by Ozme's tanks, by his choosing to follow the maxim and attack got his unit killed before time."

Noskcaj was able to make better decisions based on new information received from men who retreated from the right. Four man made decisions that day, two immortal leaders (Noskcaj and Ozme) and two of their mortal generals (Commander Noel and General Wons).

It was important to mention that making a decision is better than not making a decision at all. So the question is what decision did Ozme's general make?

CHAPTER 15 – DRINK FROM A RIVER

It was an emergency situation, every conventional treatment towards changing the systems in which man lived have been compromised. Exposure to ultraviolet radiation had been demonstrated in an array of randomized control trials to significantly reduce fatigue levels at this point and everyone was looking for water.

The first thing every soldier from Noskcaj's side did was to drink water from a river in the mountains. If you're desperate you may be able to drink the water straight from a river without doing yourself too much harm, but everyone was more than desperate, they were dying.

Information about the river was withheld by Ozme, telling no-one about the health and state of the river system. It also tells us about the sorts of impact that a river system can absorb. This information helped him manage and reduce the number of his enemies.

He dropped a sample of the T4LD into the stream before the war started, an idea proposed by his general.

He shouted: "With our river's understanding us we can set goals and decide on actions and steps for achieving a desired universe, and the enemy shall become followers like everyone else."

Noskcaj knew that something was wrong. He knew that Ozme had been repeatedly ruled out as a primary source toward him being deified... It is hard to imagine why anyone familiar with the river's history would ever decide to use it even as a temporary water source.

Noskcaj knew that Ozme was familiar with the area, and he knew Ozme was a spy, but his soldiers were not like him. He never thought Ozme was capable of poisoning a body of water flowing within the banks of different channels towards his birthplace.

At this point it was unclear as to what was about to transpire, but as Noskcaj was standing by the river's edge his horse approached him, shot, stabbed and bitten. He touched it on its head it started walking backwards in to the river. He followed it and they both disappeared under.

Noskcaj's men stood there watching, confused and every time they looked back, Ozme's men were charging. They followed their hearts and everyone started jumping into the river going after their leader but Noskcaj together with his horse havd disappeared. As Ozme's army approached, the water started bubbling and rose to the sky. Every river rose to the sky. Ozme's armies stopped. Confused, scared and amazed at the same time, everyone looked to the sky and there he was, Noskcaj on the top of the last mountain, on his horse and looking straight down into Ozme's eyes.

As everyone froze looking into the sky, the two men walked towards each other. They got close and Ozme started the conversation. "How is it that you are still alive, I watched you burn on that mountain, the power of all the painting is with me now, how is it that you're alive, how did you do all these things? Why are you alive? Unless there was one more painting you hid from me, there is no way you are walking at this present time."

"This world belongs to no-one but everyone," Noskcaj replied. "Do you know what *"THE ARTISTIC SPY"* is? It is a world created by a single mind - my mind. The capacity to self-teach, the art I create has incalculable value with prolonged observations. *"THE ARTISTIC SPY"* is created with an intention to transmit ideas in a form of irony and possibility. It does not favour any perplexed conscience minds.

I have warned you before, friend, but I have never told this, the place you come from is different from any other place anywhere. We are here at that place now and in this place you were born you poisoned the people who brought you up, in this place you will die and your existence will perish. If you look close at *"THE ARTISTIC SPY"*, it is built around a mountain, a river and land separate from each other. Now ask yourself, who is the man sitting on that chair?"

CHAPTER 16 – RELIVING THE POWER OF PURE LOVE

There was one woman who knew that deep inside him Ozme was intrinsically evil. She lived by the sea surrounded by four mountains. On one mountain there was a bridge and under it there was a waterfall.

In all the lands there were no communities, just a few people, and so much happiness reigned there. No-one knew the reason for their happiness in the land of Mostrit and none of the people were ever able to discover it. The fact of the matter was that Ozme was from this place but unlike the others, Ozme had no need for significance, he had no identity and he grew up not knowing who he was and why he was differently unhappy like the others. He had one thing in common with everyone there and that is the love for this place. After throwing Noskcaj into the lava Ozme returned to Mostrit and when he got there the population had grown significantly.

The elders recognised him as he passed through the streets with his man and they whispered: "I knew this day would come; I knew he would return".

Gossip spread around until reaching Ozme's family, memories of failure swam around inside all of their heads and knew that they needed to act before he reached the house.

In their care they had a woman who came to them years ago looking for her brother. They knew that he was back to rule and take over the land as they have heard he has done throughout his destination and his journey back home. This woman was not from there, so they had to hide her.

He marched in, stared at his aging father sitting on the sofa and out another next room came out his mother and sister. "My son," she said as she approached him.

"Mother, father."

"You are back," his father said as he stood up.

"Yes, I am back, and I am here to reclaim what is rightfully mine."

"And what is that?" his father asked.

"I am Ruler as the Lord of Mostrit and I want you both to acknowledge my right to rule the community."

"There has never been a ruler here son, even our ancestors who founded this place never declared themselves as rulers of Mostrit," his mother replied.

"Son, we have heard about what you have done to other lands. We have been shamed by our son killing and declaring himself ruler of the universe. They say he has inherited never-before-seen power and the worst was the killing of his best friend by throwing him into a mountain full of boiling lava. You will not destroy this place as you have others in our name," his father replied.

Ozme ordered the two men who were with him to stand outside, his sister approached him and tried to give him a hug. He looked at her and shoved her aside. "I am not here to ask, and for a Lord to be a Lord he has to not have a father. If he is to have a father his father must be the ruler and a Lord before him, so I am giving you a choice father. Declare me as ruler of Mostrit or I will kill every living soul in this place and take it anyway. Save your people."

Ozme's mother looked at him, tears flowing from her eyes, and said to his father: "Indob, do it. Please. For the sake of our people, we knew and the elders have warned us that something like this was to happen one day."

Ozme looked at them and said: "As I arrived here I heard there was someone living with you now, where is she, who is she?"

"There is no one, you have become worst brother!" his sister replied.

"I will find her, and I will kill her, whoever she is, as she is not from here. You will announce to the world my rule tomorrow morning father," said Ozme as he walked out the door. He then ordered his men to track down the woman who has been living with his family.

The soldiers raided the family house and found nothing, but she was captured outside Mostrit and brought to Ozme. The woman was brimming with pure love. Ozme was from this place and knew the effects of his land, but to come across an outsider who had this much love was very rare.

She looked at him and he immediately felt like she poured out the happiness he rejected since he was born. He began to be filled with feeling of love as well and couldn't help but then brim over with charity. But in a blink of a moment he remembered his purpose and thought she was going to seek to fill all others including his men with this spell.

He then called his most trusted man and ordered that she be locked away until he decides on what to do with her. He also ordered that his family be questioned about this mysterious woman and where she is from.

The next morning his father announced his son's arrival in Mostrit. "Good morning to all, today I am here to announce to you the monarch, the new head of all states, the new ruler of all lands, all kingdoms are his to do as he pleases. He now takes the title of commander of all armies and conqueror of all that lives." His father's entreaty began as a gesture of loyalty and fealty, but as he looked at his son he couldn't bear the thought of Ozme responsible for billions of lives, so he changed his tact.

"I stand in front of you all today as a father of this man. I watched him grow different from everyone else, I have always known that I made a ruthless, evil creature and if anyone out there has the will to fight against this monster I made, please fight!"

Before he could finish his speech, Ozme came behind him and stabbed his own father in the back.

"Lords do not have Makers," he said as he famously left his coronation, leaving his own father in a pool of blood and his mother and sister screaming and crying with Indon's head on their knees.

Ozme went straight to the mysterious woman kept captive and on his way there he was informed that the identity of this woman had surfaced, He learned that this woman was from Opelomag and the sister of Noskcaj.

Ozme was furious that the sister of his enemy has arrived in his birth-place and stayed for years with his family and as he walked there all which was in his head was how he was going to kill this woman. An idea came to mind that he would kill her, but when he got there she was gone, together with the men who were guarding her.

CHAPTER 17 – EFFECTIVE HEIR TO MOSTRIT

The situation that made this world created someone who has no emotions, but it was a creation fit for a ruler. "I have been patient and ready to blow." It was now time to find out who would be the next ruler of Mostrit.

Ozme has already declared himself the rightful ruler and had conquered the land without challenge, but there was one downside. Noskcaj has followed him there.

Noskcaj have never seen Mostrit before, but when he first laid eyes on the place he immediately knew that this is the place he painted in his mysterious painting. He was so shocked by the perfection of his drawing and painting something that was just an imagination to him but here he is looking at it!

He spoke to himself in a low voice with his soldiers behind him. "This is the place; I have seen the miracles the paintings can do, the paintings have been able to show me things I have never thought I will see, but this I have seen before I ever thought of creating them. Did I create this place by imagination? I feel different."

As he and his men walked toward the mountains of Mostrit they saw Ozme's army in formations. It was not Noskcaj's plan to fight in this place, he valued it so much that he wouldn't even risk the thought of seeing rubble flying all over.

On the other side Ozme didn't care if the place was destroyed. It was a ruin and his army was ready. Noskcaj retreated to the jungles of Gezina outside Mostrit; it was there that he decided to call on Ozme. Ozme agreed to the invitation of finishing the war in the jungle, and sent a message of his own.

"I have your sister and I will kill her unless you submit to me and follow any instruction I say. It is time we settled this on our own. These men will die. We started this and one of us must end it. I now possess power unimaginable to the human eye, I have the power to alter the past."

They agreed to meet by the waterfall, next to the Pride Rock.

There was a dancing woman on top of the mountain, a man sneaking and peeking from behind the trees and there was one man who never moved. This man was facing to the right without movement, the man hiding behind the trees kept hurting himself, the trees were full of dead thorns. The dancing woman kept on dancing to the sounds of birds, the bird sang and sang non-stop. But these were not songs, these were birds fighting and arguing. It is hard to image all these things happening in one place at one time.

The birds knew that danger was closing in and coming straight to Pride Rock. This is where all birds in the area gather for their slumber every morning.

The dancing woman came to the bridge above the waterfall every morning to dance and every morning there was a man hiding in the trees watching the woman dance. The man has been pierced by the thorns of the trees every morning to a point where it doesn't hurt anymore, and the poisons contained in the thorns correspond with his immune system. But there is a man who has been spotted in one place either day or night, and this man was always in the same position doing the same thing, looking to his right-hand side.

Noskcaj said: "I am warning you for the last time, Ozme. please don't do this, you will destroy everything that exists. These trees surrounding us are very dangerous trees and I have seen this in my thoughts one of us is going to fall victim to them."

"I'm powerful now. I am immune to all types of poison. I have killed myself too many times to test my immortality and nothing works, nothing can kill me. Everyone was asked to leave when it became public that the men will no longer be fighting but only the two leaders will square off in the centre of Mostrit, but no one wanted to leave and when the young once heard that their elders will not be leaving they too decided they will stay."

Noskcaj's armies returned to Mostrit. Ozme's armies stood aside and let them pass and made their way to the east, while Ozme's moved west. The two leaders had not been spotted by anyone in the last 14 hours, everyone was nervous and panicking.

Everyone wanted to see how this story of two men, one born in this land with evil in his head and the other with good trying to figure out what this place could mean to him. There started to be rumours that the two men had left and went to fight elsewhere, others thought that they had already fought and Ozme has won.

As dawn broke they all started to see sunlight, there was 44 million people surrounding the mountain and this included the soldiers and the citizens. One small boy pointed up and said "Look over there!" As they all looked they saw a woman wearing a long dress and dancing on the bridge above the waterfall on top of the mountain.

CHAPTER 18 – THE RULES YOU FOLLOWED GOT YOU HERE, NEMESIS

"You know very well that our world is changing, and that authority needs to wash itself out. It will make itself look attractive after me and you are done. We are about to reduce a most delicate, political and sociological situation to half; so ask yourself what exactly we did. The disarming smiles will not get past me on this day."

Instead, Ozme sent a scorching look to Noskcaj and replied: "Most people like to shoot guns but we don't need guns. I don't know how you have survived but today you will be lying on this rock. Today these people will witness the brutality of your creations. Many thanks must go to you for showing me a way even God can't imagine. What's holding you back? I am ready, we both have been dealing with behavioural problems and incredible results are about to come out."

"My Art has never depicted military excitement and my incomplete piece shows the prisoners being led away and animals feasting on the dead. Those soldiers down there have been scaling the walls for us, but my work appears to have been inconclusive. We had a large and dramatic battle during which you have been copying a lost painting. You might have the portrait orientation scales, but I am the master of landscape art. To recreate this bloody event, we will both have to go into that past. All my paintings are accurate historical accounts, and an impression of the uprising. In contrast to most wars which serve commemorative purposes." Noskcaj is now at ease, he is now able to wear him down; he now managed to make Ozme appear at places to which he must hasten and move swiftly where he does not expect.

Ozme's general advanced without coveting fame and his thoughts were to protect his country and do good service for his sovereign, as he made his people believe. Now Ozme knows that he can win with ease. To a surrounded enemy, you must leave a way of escape. Now he can attack his enemy direct. Ozme's main aim is to steal, kill, and destroy. That's his goal, and he will stop at nothing to accomplish it.

"The rule of this age has blinded the minds of the unbelievers; everything you believed in violates relational rules and is considered to be a negative violation of expectations."

"It is critical to understand that rules are important and not only are they made by human beings but by God himself since the beginning of Time. Rules have been used to protect the weak, a lot of people become disadvantaged if rules are broken. I have created something that questions the first rule made, but since I saw what I created I saw my creations providing a stable environment and human co-existence in ways unimaginable. I saw peace and development from new positive rules. I created my art for the sole purpose of looking into the past, to understand the existence and activities of my grandfather's father."

But to Ozme, there shall be no order, to him the pictures were created for him and only he is worthy of using them. He believes that because he has shared ideas with Noskacj in the past during their friendship stages. He had said something that led Noskcaj to creating the paintings, he believes he was the idea to creating the paintings indirectly.

"My whole life has been dedicated to obtaining confidential information without the permission of the holder of that information. Code breaking was overwhelming since I saw your work. I managed to access the place where the desired information is stored within your art and I have never excluded myself from being treated as spy. Yes, I have heard about your profession and I know the rules you follow to perform your tasks. I quietly observed. This includes an inherent deceptive trait. You have never really mastered the art of compromise. Your missions were never aborted even when you knew you failed. Your pride helped me formulate alternative solutions and you never knew when to get out. Your biggest mistake was assuming that we were friends, when you told me of all the secret spying missions you have ever done. You have believed all these years that you are a perfect spy, but that title belongs to me."

CHAPTER 19 – REBORN AT PLANET AIROTERP

In essence, the concept of living starts and will bring a new life in Mostrit; it will bring in a different physical form. The city of Mostrit will continue to exist but it will create within itself a new soul transcendent of interconnected cycles of existence.

It was mentioned before that the pictures contained T4LP which was intended to give individuals the capability to influence a change in behaviour; but it was not mentioned which one contained that effect.

In Chapter 7 Noskcaj received a letter with the words "What is hard and how hard do I work? The problem with being loyal to a course is that the course will always betray you, I am Number 4 and I am a necessity to the power of invention."

The specialists who were researching the T4LP discovered that this letter was written 444 years ago by a man called Pheri as his signature was invisibly written on the back of the letter. His records were never found, no matter how hard they tried, but they found a very crucial clue and that was this was a man no one really knew but he was a man who went to war and never came back.

Noskcaj decided to pull that letter out to see if he can understand its contents, so he read it backwards, removed certain words and twisted everything around. It now reads as follows: "Innovation of Power will always betray the course, and the work I did and how I did it was a necessity to loyal 4 numbers."

Oen heard stories about a man who was thrown into the volcano but appeared back on earth as a different person. This man created a legendary era, a man who formed existence without limitation and when he heard that this man was called Noskcaj he decided to ride to Mostrit.

After reading the letter in a different format he started having thoughts of previous existences, and that these existences were once owned by someone fighting in a war. It has always been known that there is no permanent self and that the there is no life in an independent body.

This was revealed to be false after Oen discovered that Noskcaj's second name was Pheri. When he arrived in Mostrit, he found it difficult to find Noskcaj as the soldiers restricted anyone from moving through the line further to where were Noskcaj was squaring off with Ozme.

He demanded to speak to one of the generals in Noskcaj's army and finally got through. He told him he was a lifelong friend to Noskcaj and he had vital information.

When Noskcaj looked up, Ozme was still replying to him about who the perfect spy was. He saw a woman in a red dress with yellow stripes and the words: "Will we live while we live", started a song in his mind. And he thought to himself "I don't know you, but I love you."

But to Ozme the dance was a sign, it was communication that only he was able to read. She was explaining through dance to Ozme the life of Noskcaj. This was Retina and next to her was a wooden basket with a baby inside.

She couldn't stop dancing, but she finally looked down and there she saw Noskcaj. She jumped from the bridge and killed herself immediately after looking into Noskcajs eyes, hitting the rock at the bottom and landing beside the two men. She couldn't live with the thought of betraying him.

"She was like my Art, they are both beautiful they both created deprivation of unconscious thoughts, now I may never see her again. I loved her, but I don't blame her, I only blame myself for creating useless hope."

If she is dead then who is the woman standing next to Noskcaj in *"THE ARTISTIC SPY"*? Noskcaj decided to climb the mountain to where Retina was dancing and there he found a baby in a basket. While he was there Oen saw an opportunity to go around and meet him. He told him that the letter he received was from his ancestor who he was named after.

"I am saying thank you to a man who died years before I was born," but what he did not know was that he was saying thank you to himself.

Oen also told Noskcaj that this child belonged to him, and that both Retina and the baby were brought to Mostrit by his sister. Right there Noskcaj named the baby Nadroj.

"His fathers before him have worked to greater purpose, a child born in Airoterp." While he was up there on the mountain Ozme instructed his soldiers to attack everyone not loyal to him, but his soldiers had a change of heart, they were now drawn to Noskcaj's cause.

Ozme shouted from the bottom of the waterfall. "This is the start of harmful action against everyone; I will hurt all of you for rejecting my existence. I know how it will happen, I have seen it, but give me this moment to display to you my existence. A day will come when this world will believe and think that you are all safe and happy, and suddenly your days will become dark and the emotion called love will turn to ashes, and you'll know that existence existed in my hands. You will know that I am everything and my enemies are nothing." He retreated backwards into the waterfall's cave.

CHAPTER 20 – THE LAST MARVEL ARTIST

When the walls fell and the cave closed, everyone's hearts were filled with joy, but the last inch in him shall not free everyone.

Paintings are an expression on feelings and emotions, showing us what we see inside us. Trapped inside the cave he felt the need to create his own painting and named it "Blue lights see everything".

A few years passed and everyone had forgotten his existence. Noskcaj became adviser to the community, refusing to be crowned ruler of Mostrit as long as Ozme's body was never found. As Noskcaj sat on a chair, the community found out when the cave was closed. He thought about how the paintings have influenced his existence. He thought about his horse but when he raised his head there he was - Ozme - in front of him.

He knelt down on his left leg and in his hand, there was a sword, and he was dressed in armour. Noskcaj stood up and walked in Ozme's direction. As he walked he took off his armour and approached. As Noskcaj approached, Ozme stood up and put on his helmet, placed his sword in a fighting mode and said: "My heart is blue, it can create a river, my fingers are frozen by blue snow, my eyes are red but they cry blue water for they have doubled as diamonds, I have forged you from magic metal burned by blue fire, I composed you fresh from the earth and you shall loosen everyone's tomorrow."

Noskcaj looked up and all he could see was the blue sky. He raised his arms and said: "I have been waiting. I have been waiting for you to storm troop the carriages and pause to see anyone's tomorrow. We are both artists in our own right, your heart is filled with vengeance, and you are ready to fight. Your son awaits you. Everyone told him you are dead, but I told him you are alive. I expose myself to your weapon."

Noskcaj walked back, sat on his chair, took a knife and cut one rose from the basket of roses behind him. Behind him walked a woman who then stood next to him. He took off his shoe and placed his left foot into a small pool full of fish.

"I am ready to die; I have been part of a dream that can never exist, Ozme. I tried to lead someone else's life, I have tried to live my grandfather's life, so I took his story and made it mine and, in the process, I created you. It's a hard life. When you were away I didn't know how I was going to make it, and somehow, I am still breathing. I have no-one to believe in and there is nothing inside me anymore. It always makes me think every night is the last because when I made you it was not out of thought but from the unknown."

GALLERY

I drew these pictures not knowing if they will take me anywhere but my passion led me to their completion and their completion led me to writing this book. My passion for art started at a very early age but writing a book was not one of my goals.

THE TEMPTATION

WHERE DO YOU THINK YOU COME FROM?

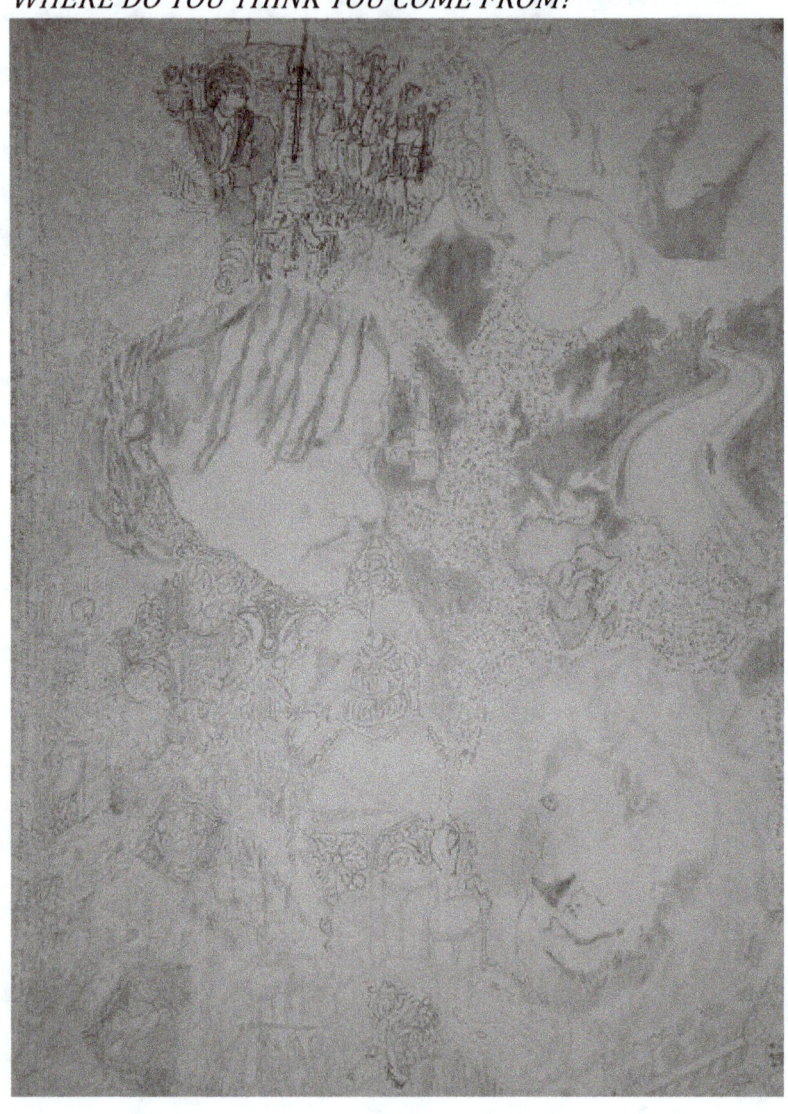

ABOUT THE AUTHOR

This book is written by Mampheri Jackson Malepo, owner and director of MJM Auto Services and Battery Station, Midrand.

Jackson holds an honours degree in Business Management and Industrial Psychology.

A black conscious South African from Limpopo.

The book's journey started with him drawing pictures whilst in University. Later he wrote a story around the drawings.

He still intends to turn the pictures into paintings and sculpture the chair featured in one of the drawings.